WATCH OVER HER

'I don't like men who say they're from the water company and come inside your flat,' said Anne.

There were no more games. The children didn't seem to like Mrs Cattermole's story. Soon they left and Mrs Cattermole heard their voices softly die away.

WATCH OVER HER

Titles in the series *On Target*:

6000 WORDS

Cuts Deep by Catherine Johnson

Dragonwood by Alex Stewart

Off the Rails by Anne Rooney

3000 WORDS | ILLUSTRATED

Soldier Boy by Anne Rooney

Watch over her by Dennis Hamley

WATCH OVER HER

Dennis Hamley

ReadZone Books Limited
50 Godfrey Avenue
Twickenham
TW2 7PF
www.ReadZoneBooks.com

Originally published by Evans Brothers Ltd, London in 2009.

Design: Nicolet Oost Lievense
Cover design: Jurian Wiese
Images: iStockphoto
Printed by Easy-to-Read Publications

British Library Cataloguing in Publication Data (CIP) is available
for this title.

ISBN 978 1 78322 085 4

Contents

Chapter One

The Alderman Wix estate was grey, forlorn and almost deserted. Soon the demolition men would move in.

Not yet though. The blocks of flats with their cracked concrete walkways and dripping walls could not be knocked down until the last stubborn old people had been cleared out. Only a few had clung on, but they were so difficult to rehouse. The two men who were walking round it one morning knew this and also that there wasn't much time left.

'How are we going to do it?' said one. 'We can't go knocking on every door.'

'Listen and learn,' said the other as an old man shuffled by leaning on a stick. He went up to him.

'Excuse me, guv'nor. Could you tell me where Mrs Freakwell lives?

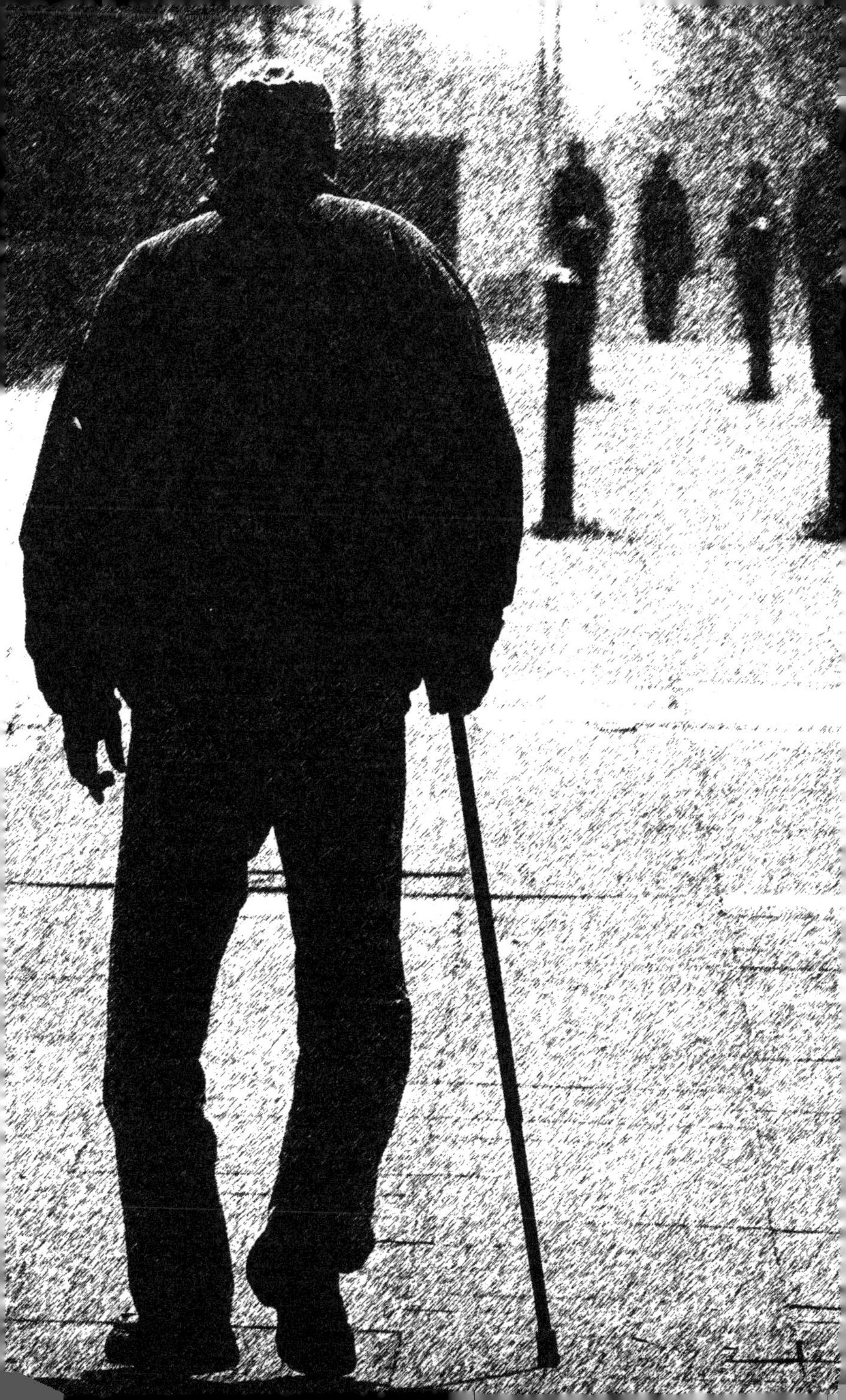

Only we're her nephews and we haven't seen her for years. We'd like to have a chat with her before they knock this place down.'

'Freakwell?' said the old man. 'Nobody round here with that name. I'd know if there was 'cos I never heard a name like that.'

'I suppose I might have got it wrong. It's been a long time. I know she lives here somewhere. Try a few more names.'

'Well, there's the Ellises at number fifteen and the Smiths at twelve. Let me see, who else is there?'

'Who lives over there?' The man

jerked his thumb towards a flat which looked dingier than the rest. Dirty curtains hung behind the windows: the once-blue door looked forlorn as if nobody ever visited.

'Ah, that's Mrs Cattermole at number twenty-nine. Weird one, she is. She don't come out much nowadays, but when she does she says a lot of strange things. Nobody takes any notice though. We've heard it all before.'

'Such as?'

'Well, she keeps on about some treasure she's got. "Nobody knows about my treasure," she says. I say,

"If you don't stop blabbin' about it everyone's goin' to know and there may be people among 'em you wouldn't want to." But she doesn't seem to understand. "My children know all about it," she says. "They won't tell anyone."'

'Children?'

'Daft old bat. There are no children. There haven't been children round here since – well, there aren't no children. She's ravin'. She ought to be in a home.'

'I reckon I did get the name wrong. It's that Mrs Cattermole who's our auntie. I knew her name ended with an 'l'. We'll go off and have a cup of tea and then we'll go and see her. Thanks mate.'

The old man watched them go. 'Nice lads, thinking about their old auntie,' he said to himself.

The children often came to see Mrs Cattermole. If they were late, she would pull her frayed shawl tighter, huddle nearer to the heatless hearth and pray that they would soon arrive. It was strange that the moment she finished her prayers, they always appeared as if someone had called them.

First she heard their clear piping voices, then tinkly laughter and, last of all, skipping footsteps as they gathered round her. One might take her hand and hold it in a grip so light that it was as if she was brushed by a feather, another might stroke her thinning hair with fingers that hardly touched. All the children would look down on her tenderly, lovingly.

Then they would break away and play the games she knew so well. There were dipping games, tig, hop-scotch, skipping to rhymes she clapped her old, wrinkled, veiny

hands to. She longed to go further and join in. Sometimes she thought she succeeded. She left her chair by the fireplace. Her body was suppler, lighter. The children looked up to her and their eyes shone with gratitude and love. She felt so young again, so happy.

Then as suddenly as they came, they were gone and she was back in the shell of old age.

'You'd look a bit silly if there *had* been a Mrs Freakwell there.'

'No chance. Have you ever heard a name like that?'

They were in a Macdonalds nearby eating burgers.

'What do we do now then?'

There was only one leader in this twosome and he had no doubts.

'We try the water company trick.'

'But we're always doing the water company trick.'

'Yeah, because it works. These old grunters fall for it every time. Besides, this one's really worth it now the old bloke's told us she's got a treasure.'

'He might be as daft as she is. And we don't know what the treasure is.'

'I know he looks a bit doolally, but I reckon he knows what he's talkin' about. And it's obvious what it is. Money stashed away in a pillowcase. Some of these old biddies are loaded. We'll take a look this afternoon and come back for it later.'

'What if she won't let it go? We might have to thump her.'

'Then we thump her. It's all the same to me.'

The two men finished their coffee.

'Time to go,' said the leader.

Chapter Two

Mrs Cattermole knew all their names. First was little, fair-haired Rosie, always laughing. She could skip so fast that Mrs Cattermole was dizzy watching the rope fly round and her little feet dance over it. Sometimes she sang, softly, as if her voice came from millions of miles away, songs her father taught her when he came home from the sea. But he would teach her no more, because one day he did not return.

Then there was Jimmy, tall, wiry, with dark eyes and sticking-out ears. He could run faster, climb higher and throw further than anyone else. Next was quiet Anne with the plaits. She played with her dolls on her own but never cried when Alec and Tom teased her and ran off with her toy pram. Then there were

Michael and Barry and Susan and Ruthie and so many more – and they all came to see old Mrs Cattermole, every day.

One day, after the games were played, the children clustered round her bed and said, 'Tell us a story please.'

But Mrs Cattermole was too old now to remember any stories. So she told them about things which had happened to her instead.

'Two men from the water company came this afternoon. Nice young men they were. They said they had to check a tap in my bedroom cupboard. I've never seen a tap there, but they said it was a very small one and not everybody knew about it, but it's so important that if it goes wrong all the water will be cut off.'

'But that's the cupboard where you keep your treasure,' said Jimmy.

'Oh bless you,' said Mrs Cattermole. 'I know what you're thinking. But they were both so nice and they wouldn't dream of taking my treasure. It's still there, just as I left it. And they told me they'd mended the tap so it was all right now and they were sorry for bothering me.'

'I don't like men who say they're

from the water company and come inside your flat,' said Anne.

There were no more games. The children didn't seem to like Mrs Cattermole's story. Soon they left and Mrs Cattermole heard their voices softly die away.

Something was wrong. The children had not been happy but she couldn't quite grasp why. She stood up, walked to the cupboard and searched inside.

Darkness had fallen. A dead, cold wind sighed round the crumbling stairs and walkways. Nobody heard two pairs of training shoes padding along or saw their sinister wearers.

'I can't remember where it is in this dark.'

'Twenty-nine. Second floor. You were only 'ere this morning. Gimme the torch.'

'Are you sure you know what you're doin'?'

'Trust me.'

'I got her pension book while you were gropin' round that cupboard. Ain't that enough from the old girl's pad?'

'I keep tellin' you, these old people, they've no idea what they've got.

There's a big tin box in that cupboard and I want to know what's in it. While I was pretendin' to find the tap, she was mutterin' to herself about nobody should touch her treasure.'

'She should be so lucky.'

'You know what I reckon?'

'No? What?'

'That treasure's in the box. I want that box. I want that treasure, whatever it is. So come on. Gimme that torch, I said.'

The same frigid wind pushed into their faces as they crept along the walkway. The torch shone at successive doors. Thirty-one …

thirty … twenty-nine.

'This is it. She'll be kippin' by the fire'.

He wedged an iron bar between door and frame. A quick pull, a splinter and the flimsy lock gave way. They were inside.

Chapter Three

Mrs Cattermole stirred.

'Jimmy?' she called softly. 'Rosie? Barry?'

'It's all right, Ma,' said a voice she thought she knew. 'It's only us from the water company again. We've still got a bit to do on that tap. Is it all right if we get on with it?'

Mrs Cattermole didn't answer. But deep in her mind she could hear Anne's voice. '*I don't like men who say they're from the water company.*'

The men opened the cupboard.

'What a stink,' said one. 'I never noticed it this afternoon. These old hags should be put down.'

'Shut up and hold the torch so I can see in the cupboard.'

A moment passed, then, angrily, '*It's gone.*'

Mrs Cattermole cried, 'Where are

you? I can't see you.'

Suddenly the torch was turned full in her face, blinding her.

'That's all right, Grandma,' said the torch-bearer. 'You stay where you are. We'll be gone in a minute.'

The other hissed, '*Look*. She's clutchin' the treasure herself.'

'Who are you? I don't believe you're from the water company. Where's my Jimmy? Where's my Susan? Where's Tom?'

'Give us the box, love. You know it makes sense. You'll get hit else.'

Mrs Cattermole got out of her chair, clutched the box tightly and

cowered back into a corner.

'Give us the box, I said. I don't want to have to hit you.'

'You're not my children. Where are my children?'

'Give it 'ere.'

'I don't know who you are.' Mrs Cattermole's knotted fingers still stubbornly clutched the box to her thin body.

'Right, darlin', that's it.' He raised the iron bar and pulled her out of her chair. 'I didn't want to do this but it looks like you've made me, Grandma.'

If anyone ever spoke to the children – which wasn't possible because nobody knew they were there – and asked them why they kept coming to see Mrs Cattermole, they would say that one day Mrs Cattermole would need their help. Rosie saw first that the time had come.

'Quick,' she cried. 'It's happening now.'

Jimmy appeared by her side.

'They're going to hurt her,' he cried. 'She needs us.'

To the men it seemed as if a sudden black cloud of angry wasps enveloped them. One dropped the iron bar, the other the torch. They flailed their hands and arms desperately to be clear of them but they settled all over their bodies. Yet there were no stings: instead they felt the sharp feel of tiny human teeth biting into their legs, little fingers with long nails scratching their arms and faces, miniature fists tugging on what was left of hair on their shaven heads. They stopped pulling at Mrs Cattermole's fiercely clutched treasure and blindly staggered away from her.

Then the air cleared, the wasps

disappeared and the two men stared at what they saw.

Mrs Cattermole was back in her chair. The box was open and her treasure was scattered over the floor. When they saw what they had done all this for, both men felt sudden shame and foolishness. But far more than this they felt sudden stark fear, for children had come from nowhere to surround Mrs Cattermole, stroking her hair, caressing her cheeks and speaking softly and consolingly.

Anne kissed her on the forehead and said, 'You're all right now.'

Susan bent down, picked up and

replaced everything in the box and gave it back to Mrs Cattermole.

'Have a little sleep,' said Ruthie.

The boys turned round and Tom said, 'We haven't finished.' The girls left Mrs Cattermole and joined them. Their eyes, suddenly hard and cold, stared straight at the thieves, who were caught immoveably in a laser beam of determined hatred.

Mrs Cattermole leant back and closed her eyes. She felt marvellously at peace. The children would make everything all right. They always had and always would.

Chapter Four

It was ridiculous. The children were running at them from all sides. They kicked ankles, knees, calves. They gripped hands and wrists like tiny but immensely strong vices. They bit arms with sharp and deadly teeth, so purple marks suffused with blood appeared on their skin like aeroplanes in formation. A tall, thin boy whirled something small and hard on a string round his head: it crashed into a shaven temple with the force not of a mere conker but a meteorite. A girl jabbed a thigh with a needle, driving it hard through denim, flesh and muscle and the man howled in agony.

A boy and a girl pulled at the thieves' feet so that they lost their balance. There was nothing the thieves could do. They were pulled through the door, out on to the walkway where the cold, dead wind hit them clammily. Then these superhumanly strong kids pushed them further towards the edge. They felt cold steel railings at their backs and knew they were now held at bay.

For the first time they saw the children clearly. The boys all wore white shirts and grey flannel shorts with rucked-up socks. The girls wore print cotton dresses and leather sandals. They took all this in and looked at each other. There was no need to speak. They couldn't have this: they couldn't be bested by kids.

If children had to be bludgeoned with iron then so be it.

They struck out wildly, hitting nothing. The iron bar dropped on the floor. Somehow they dragged the weight of the children away from the railings. And yet it seemed as though the children were allowing them to do it, as if they were making space for a final assault.

And then suddenly there were no children round their feet. Instead, they were standing in front of them, looking at them intensely: strange, enigmatic, unblinking, pale-eyed stares which chilled their souls. They recognised contempt and accusation which struck deep into their very souls and never wavered, so it seemed time had stopped and would never start again. The thieves could only watch and wait for the next move, if there was ever to be one.

Then something changed.

Mrs Cattermole sighed, a sigh of complete contentment. Now she knew she would be safe for ever. Her children had not let her down. She knew they wouldn't. How many years had they been there when she needed them? More than her tired old mind could begin to remember. Ah well, there was no need for them any more now. Her head sank back and she entered a peace which would never be broken again.

Sheerest nightmare. Time was going backwards. The children's clothes started to decay. White shirts and grey shorts mouldered on them. Colourful print dresses turned to sere and grey. Myriad holes appeared in cloth and made it a strange and strengthless lace. Mildew, ragged and green, streaked and spotted it.

Shoes disintegrated.

Yet the young faces still stared. The children raised their hands and pointed, as if cursing the men. Those hands grew thin, became claws, sticks, bones. Flesh melted from faces. Sparkling eyes dulled, disappeared and round black sockets gaped in their place. Mouths stretched in triumphant smiles, then lengthened further into deaths' heads grins which leered under holes where nostrils were.

The small skeletons in rags surrounded the thieves. For an appalling moment they stood

silently jeering. Then they collapsed for the lack of life in them. Small piles of bones, skin, nails and hair ringed the thieves and covered their shoes with dust.

The men howled wordlessly, animals in terror. Their cries brought out even those who had barred the doors vowing not to show themselves before morning. Afterwards, everyone agreed on what they had seen and heard. There was a metallic creaking and rending as the railings gave way. Two bodies dropped two floors and sprawled awkwardly on the cracked asphalt.

But there was nothing and nobody on the walkway. There was no reason for these sudden panicked falls.

Chapter Five

Arc lights glared into every corner of the estate. An ambulance waited under the broken railings. Four police cars stood nearby. Their radios crackled and muttered.

Knots of frightened tenants told
what little they knew to policemen.
The two broken bodies under
the walkway were examined and
pronounced dead.

A man's voice called out, 'In here, sir.'

It came from the open door of flat twenty-nine on the second floor. A detective in a brown topcoat ran up the stairway and joined the detective constable.

'Look,' said the constable.

A scene of threadbare misery lit by a single 40-watt bulb. Not for the first time in his life, the inspector prayed he wouldn't end up like that. In a chair by a fireplace, empty except for an old two-bar electric fire with only one bar working, sat an old woman, leaning back, an expression of serene happiness on her face.

'I think she's dead, sir,' said the constable.

'We'd better get the paramedics up to check,' said the inspector.

'Natural causes, I reckon,' said the constable. 'Only a few minutes ago too. If she's dead, she's still warm. As far as anyone can be in this place.'

'So there are no marks on her?'

'None that I can see.'

'Anything else?'

'Yes, sir. Signs of forced entry.' He picked up the iron bar. 'They got in with this. Makes a good weapon too.'

'So the three deaths are connected,' said the inspector, looking back, into the night. 'Extraordinary.'

'Sir?'

'Those thugs came here to rob her. But they didn't hit her and didn't get away with anything. And now they're dead in the ambulance. I just don't get it.'

The inspector looked down on Mrs Cattermole. 'I was talking to one of the tenants. She told me there was a rumour that she had some sort of treasure stashed away. Our dead friends must have heard the rumours and tried their luck.'

'They got more than they bargained for,' said the constable.

'Hello, what's this?' said the inspector.

He prised a printed tin box away from her hands and clicked the lid open. On top was money – a few notes held with an elastic band, some pound and fifty pence coins. There was also other money, large and heavy copper and silver coins.

'Pre-decimal,' said the inspector. 'Hardly worth the thieves' time.'

But none of that mattered. Underneath were papers: old and

yellowing forms, certificates and newspaper cuttings. There were objects as well, unexpected and strange. Three spiral marbles. A shrivelled conker still on its string. A tin whistle. Faded black and white photographs of children. A small, velvet lined box with inside it a military medal on its ribbon. What looked like a parchment, rolled up and secured with an elastic band.

'Let's see who she was,' said the inspector. They sorted through the papers. A birth certificate: *Hilda Brown, born 1918.* A marriage

certificate: *Hilda Brown and James Cattermole, 1940.* A telegram, also dated 1940, informing her that her husband, Lance-Corporal James Cattermole, was killed in action at Dunkirk. With it was a letter with BUCKINGHAM PALACE at the top – James Cattermole had been posthumously awarded the Military Medal.

'A few great weeks, then seventy years without her husband,' the constable murmured. 'It's a big load to carry.'

The inspector didn't answer. He was reading one of the newspaper cuttings. At length he spoke.

'After her husband was killed, she worked in a children's home. This cutting is about what she did.'

'What was that?'

'The home was out in the country near an RAF airfield. There was a big raid on it. She was getting all her kids into an air-raid shelter. Most were in, but a few were still outside so she went looking for them. She was still outside the shelter when it took a direct hit. All the kids she thought she'd saved were killed.'

They were both silent for a moment, then the inspector unrolled the parchment.

The other policeman was rummaging further in the box.

'What's this?' he said, picking up a badge, more like a brooch, in the form of bronze oak leaves.

The inspector looked up from the parchment.

'It's her civilian gallantry award,' he said. 'Listen to this: "To Hilda Cattermole, who, in the service of others and regardless of her own safety…"' He stopped in mid-sentence, then said, 'This tin *is* her treasure. Her whole life's in here.'

The two men looked at the dead

old lady.

'She had a tale to tell,' said the constable.

A sergeant entered the flat.

'No sign of a struggle,' he said. 'Our two jokers seem to have gone over the top of their own accord. I'll tell you one thing though.'

'What's that, sarge?' asked the constable.

'I've been in the force twenty years and I never saw terror like I saw on those two faces.'

But the inspector was more interested in Mrs Cattermole.

'She must have loved those kids in

the children's home,' he said. 'She watched over them as best she could. Pity they couldn't have done the same for her.'

Titles in the series *On Target*

6000 WORDS

Cuts Deep
Catherine Johnson
ISBN 978 1 78322 082 3

Dragonwood
Alex Stewart
ISBN 978 1 78322 083 0

Off the Rails
Anne Rooney
ISBN 978 1 78322 081 6

3000 WORDS | ILLUSTRATED

Soldier Boy
Anne Rooney
ISBN 978 1 78322 084 7

Watch over her
Dennis Hamley
ISBN 978 1 78322 085 4